Puffin Books   *Editor: Kaye Webb*

The Penny Pony

Cathy and Roger first saw the pony in Mrs Boddy's
shop. His eye seemed to roll in a very lively manner,
and you felt that he might toss his head at any moment.
He looked almost like a real pony, but really he was
part of a large old pram.

What the children wanted most in all the world was a
real pony, but this one was very handsome, and he
cost only a penny. So they bought him and called
him Prince Penny because he was black and brave, and
Cathy looked after him every day, until one day she
came home to find he'd gone.

But after all her unhappiness she discovered that by
losing one friend she had found another one to love,
who needed even more care and love, and she knew
that Prince would understand why he had to live in a
museum.

For children of six to eight.

The Penny Pony

Barbara Willard

Illustrated by Juliette Palmer

Puffin Books

Puffin Books, Penguin Books Ltd, Harmondsworth,
Middlesex, England
Penguin Books, 625 Madison Avenue,
New York, New York 10022, U.S.A.
Penguin Books Australia Ltd, Ringwood,
Victoria, Australia
Penguin Books Canada Ltd, 2801 John Street,
Markham, Ontario, Canada L3R 1B4
Penguin Books (N.Z.) Ltd, 182–190 Wairau Road,
Auckland 10, New Zealand

First published by Hamish Hamilton 1961
Published in Puffin Books 1967
Reprinted 1971, 1972, 1978

Made and printed in Great Britain by
Hazell Watson & Viney Ltd, Aylesbury, Bucks
Set in Monotype Baskerville

Contents

1

Mrs Boddy's Shop

Cathy and her brother Roger were looking in the window of Mrs Boddy's shop, when they suddenly saw the pony.

'There!' said Cathy. 'Look! Quick!'

'Is it real?' Roger asked.

Cathy did not answer at once. She would have liked to think that the pony was a real pony, because that was the thing they both wanted most of all in the world, though they knew they could not have it. It looked real because it was at the back of the shop, and there was a door open just behind it with the winter sun streaming through. This made the pony look almost life-size to Cathy. Its eye seemed to roll in a very lively manner. If you wanted to, you could tell yourself that its black sides shone because they were well groomed, and not just because they were made of plaster and paint. At any moment, Cathy felt, the pony might toss its head.

'Is it a rocking horse?' Roger insisted. He was younger than Cathy but more practical.

'No. I don't think so.'

'Then what sort of a horse?'

'I don't know yet,' said Cathy. 'I'll ask Mrs Boddy.'

This was brave of her, for Mrs Boddy was a rather frightening person. She was all right when she was in a good mood, but there was no way of knowing whether she was likely to be in a good mood or not.

Cathy went into the shop and Roger followed rather slowly. As they stepped on the mat the bell rang furiously. They knew this would happen because they had been in the shop before – but it made them jump, all the same.

Mrs Boddy appeared in the open doorway behind the pony. She was wearing an overall, her head was tied up in a scarf, she had gloves on and she carried a broom. It was clear that she was turning out.

'Well?' she said. And they knew at once that although she was not in her worst mood, she was certainly not in her best.

They stood awkwardly among the jumble of old furniture, chipped china, brass candlesticks, dusty books and all the other amazing assortment of junk. The shop was warmed by an old oil stove that smelt, and somehow seemed to make the place colder instead of warmer.

'It's that pony,' Cathy said at last, pointing. 'We wondered about it.'

'I don't see there's much wondering to be done,' Mrs Boddy said disagreeably. 'It's been stuck away for years and years. High time I turfed it out.'

'But what sort of a horse is it?' Roger insisted.

Mrs Boddy pulled at a handle and gave a great heave. Cathy and Roger saw then that the pony was part of an old pram. It was a very old-fashioned one, the sort their grandmother might have had when she was a child. It was pushed from behind and the pony was on the front, so that the pram looked like some sort of small carriage. As Mrs Boddy gave it a shove it ran forward, all its rusty parts squealing, and the pony moved up and down in a kind of rusty canter.

'Used to have reins,' Mrs Boddy explained. 'The lucky little girl who was pushed in that pram held the reins –'

'And the pony went up and down,' Cathy cried excitedly, 'like a real pony pulling a real little carriage!'

'Or it could have been a lucky little boy,' said Roger.

Mrs Boddy laughed and began to sound more friendly. 'So it could. Not much of it left now, is

there? Tyres gone, handle broken, sides scratch-ed, hood torn, rust everywhere. . . .'

'Is it for sale?' asked Cathy.

'I'm putting it out for Miss Maltby. She's having one of her jumble sales and I promised I'd see what I could find.'

Miss Maltby lived a mile or so out of the country town that was home for Cathy and Roger. In her fields she had made a home for a lot of unwanted animals – horses and donkeys, stray cats and dogs, almost anything on four legs. Sometimes she found new owners for these animals, sometimes they just stayed with her. If there was a particular animal she had heard about, whose owner could no longer keep it, then Miss Maltby would get up a jumble sale and try to get enough money to buy that ani-mal.

Cathy was looking almost fierce. Roger knew she was screwing up her courage to ask Mrs Boddy a question. At last, out it came.

14

'Couldn't we have it?' she asked. 'We terribly want a real pony, but we'll never be able to have one. It's too much money and there's nowhere but the garden to keep it and they won't let us.'

'I should think not!' cried Mrs Boddy. 'That lovely garden!'

'This is the best un-real pony I have ever seen,' Cathy went on. 'Because of how you could rush about with it. And because even when it squeaks it sounds a bit like whinnying.'

'You'd better go to the jumble sale, then, and buy it.'

'How much would it be?'

'Not much more than a penny, by the looks of it.'

'But it's bound to be on a Saturday – jumble sales always are. I have to go to Brownies on Saturday mornings, and Roger's always being dragged off to have his hair cut. We'd never get there in time. Someone else would get it.'

'Some lucky little boy,' said Roger gloomily.

Mrs Boddy began to look cross again. 'You know very well I never give things away – it's more than my life's worth. Do it once, and I'll have half the kids in the town on my doorstep. No. Sorry.'

Cathy frowned. She could not believe that the pony would not be hers. There must be some way of getting it.

'Well,' said Roger, 'if we gave you a penny

you could give the penny to Miss Maltby instead of the pony.'

'My goodness!' cried Mrs Boddy. 'Some people can't take No for an answer. All right, then. Give me a penny and take the wretched thing away.'

Roger nearly burst with pleasure at his own cleverness in thinking of this idea, but Cathy still frowned. She pulled him on one side.

'Have you got a penny?' she asked in a whisper.

'No – but you have.'

'I haven't.'

'You must have.'

'I haven't – I haven't!' cried Cathy, sounding as though she might start to cry.

Roger seized her by the arm and pulled her towards the door.

'Thanks, Mrs Boddy!' he cried as they went out. 'We'll be back with the money later. Mind you don't go selling the pony to anyone else.'

A penny is not a lot of money, but if you have not got one it is difficult to find. The trouble for Cathy and Roger was that their mother was not at home. She had gone to London for the day, where their father's office was. There was no one they could ask for the money without getting into trouble when their parents returned and heard about it.

'We must earn it,' Cathy said. 'Where could we get a job quickly? If it was summer we could do some weeding.'

'We can go to Miss Maltby's, of course,' said Roger. 'We'll clean up her yard. Or get some feed ready. Or brush some dogs or something. I should think she'd give us a penny for that.'

Cathy was almost annoyed that she had not thought of this herself. 'Come on, then, quickly,' she cried. 'We can't waste time or Mrs Boddy might change her mind.'

'It's a very good arrangement,' Roger said. 'Miss Maltby will pay us a penny for helping

18

her, and we shall give the penny to Mrs Boddy, and she'll give it back to Miss Maltby. So everyone will be all right.'

'But mostly us,' Cathy said, as they turned down the hill and began hurrying off in the direction of Miss Maltby's house.

2

Miss Maltby

Miss Maltby lived in an old farmhouse. The house was surrounded by barns and stables and tidy sheds. These in their turn were surrounded by green fields. And the green fields were then divided from the road and from the property of neighbours by a well-kept hawthorn hedge.

In the farmhouse with Miss Maltby lived her nephew, Bob, who worked for her, seven or eight cats of different colours, four or five assorted dogs and ten budgerigars. In the sheds, some of which had neat runs, lived a variety of animals such as rabbits and hamsters and white mice. In the field several horses, ponies, donkeys and one mule enjoyed an easy life after years of hard work. Hens scratched and pecked in the farm-yard; ducks and geese squabbled by the small round pond.

As Cathy and Roger turned in at the gate and walked up to the house, they saw Miss Maltby just going into one of the stables. She had a bundle of hay under each arm. She was wearing a pair of old green slacks, gum boots covered in mud and a man's sweater. The sweater was red and her hair, which was very curly, was red, too; but it was a different red, more like orange.

'She looks like traffic lights,' said Roger. 'Only the orange ought to be in the middle.'

'Come on,' said Cathy. 'She's seen us.'

They dashed up to her. Roger tried to take one armful of hay and Cathy the other.

'We'll help you, Miss Maltby,' Cathy said.

'Let me carry it for you,' said Roger.

'Goodness me. Well.' Miss Maltby sounded most surprised. 'What's all this about?'

21

Cathy thought they had better explain without wasting time.

'Could we do a job for you?' she asked. 'We need a little money. We could carry in the hay, or sweep the yard.'

'Or we could groom a horse.'

'You'd need a ladder, Roger,' said Miss Maltby.

'Brush the dogs then,' Roger said, wheedling, and sounding like a man striking a bargain.

'I can't pay very much, you know. How much do you need?'

'Only a penny,' said Cathy.

'Two would be better,' said Roger, 'but one will do for what we want.'

'And what do you want?'

'It's something very strange and beautiful that's in Mrs Boddy's shop.'

Miss Maltby laughed. 'I don't believe there's anything beautiful in Mrs Boddy's shop.'

'We think it's beautiful,' Cathy assured her.

24

'Anyway, it's not the first beautiful thing to be there. Because there was that old stone vase Mr Richardson bought.'

Mr Richardson was a neighbour. He was extremely clever. He worked in a museum in London and he was always discovering valuable things in odd places. He bought them for a few shillings and when he had cleaned them they were seen to be rare and important, worthy of a place in the museum. Not long ago, their father had shown Cathy and Roger a long piece in the newspaper that was all about Mr Richardson. There was even a photograph, so there was no doubt about it being their Mr Richardson and no other.

'All right,' said Miss Maltby. 'if you say it's beautiful then no doubt it is. You can clean out the hamsters. A penny each – each person, I mean, not each hamster. Bob's in the end shed. He'll tell you what to do.'

With that, smiling, she went on into the stable.

Cathy and Roger hurried to the shed, and there was Bob, measuring out meal and bird seed. He was a very tall boy of about seventeen with untidy hair, red like his aunt's. He showed them where to find clean straw and sawdust and then left them to it.

'Don't forget water,' he said over his shoulder, as he went off. He never talked much.

Cleaning out the hamsters was a wonderful job. They lived in neat small houses all along one broad shelf. Each time a house was opened, the hamster inside scuttled upstairs to the bedroom. After a bit, he would peer out cautiously.

'They have such *smiles*,' said Roger.

Cathy did not say very much. On any other day she would have been as pleased and excited by the hamsters as Roger was. But she kept thinking about the pony in Mrs Boddy's shop, and where they would keep it when they got it home, and where they would take it for rides, and what they might call it.

27

'Hurry up,' she said, as Roger lingered over putting the hamsters back into their places. 'Anyway, Miss Maltby didn't say we could take them out. Suppose they suddenly ran off?'

Miss Maltby herself came into the shed just then. She must have had the same thought as Cathy, for she put her hand carefully over the hamster that was sitting close under Roger's left ear and put it quickly into its house.

28

'Have to be careful of cats,' she explained. Anyone else might have spoken rather sharply, but Miss Maltby was very sympathetic to anyone who liked handling animals.

She dug into the pocket of her green trousers and brought out two pennies.

'Here you are. One each. You'd better hurry along and buy the beautiful thing in Mrs Boddy's shop. And ask her if she's remembered about the jumble for my sale.'

'She has,' said Cathy. 'That was how we found the beautiful thing. She was turning out this morning. There's lots of junk for you.'

'Good. I need lots. I want to buy two old circus horses I've heard about. Their owner has died and nobody wants them. Perhaps your mother has some things she could let me have. Will you ask her?'

They promised. They tried to talk politely to Miss Maltby, because she was someone they liked as well as someone who had paid them

29

for working. But they were almost hopping with impatience to get back to Mrs Boddy's shop.

At last they were away. They were running down the track to the main road – they were dashing along the footpath by the side of Miss Maltby's neat hedges – they were coming at last within sight of the town. Then they were level with the first shop – then half-way up the hill – then at Mrs Boddy's door. . . .

For a moment they paused. They felt almost afraid to go inside in case after all the black shiny pony had been some sort of a dream.

'Come on,' said Cathy.

She grabbed Roger's hand. They pushed open the door, the bell rang furiously, they jumped as usual. Then they saw Mrs Boddy coming through from the room at the back. She still had a duster in her hand but this time she looked much more friendly.

'Just been giving him the once-over,' she said, dragging the pony forward. 'A penny we said, didn't we? Right. Hand over, then, and the creature's yours.'

3

A Name for the Pony

They took it in turns to push the pony home.
Mrs Boddy had very kindly put some oil on the
rusty wheels, so they were hardly squeaking at
all. Also she had oiled the shafts that fixed the
pony to the pram. The pony moved up and
down quite easily now, its neck arched, its nostrils wide and seeming to snort. When the pram
moved fast, the pony appeared to break into a
canter. The faster Cathy and Roger went, the
faster moved the pony, until the canter was
nearly a gallop.

'It's better than I thought!' Cathy cried
breathlessly, as she rushed along, Roger panting

at her heels and the pony, of course, keeping well ahead of both of them.

They had to go part of the way through the town to reach their home. People turned and looked at them as they went by. Mostly they smiled quite kindly, but a boy on a bicycle shouted out and made rude jeering noises.

Roger shouted back; Cathy managed not to.

'We'll go by the short cut,' she said, glaring at the boy and hoping that at the very least the chain would come off his bicycle.

'It's terribly steep that way,' Roger objected. 'It's rough as rough. The wheels might come off.'

'We can put them on again. I'd rather the wheels came off than have the pony laughed at.'

Roger saw that his sister was wearing what he called her furious face. Once that happened he knew very well that it saved time to do as she said. He was pushing the pony just then, so he turned off the pavement up the steep and nar-

row cutting that led away from the town and over the hill to their home.

It was hard going on the rough little track. They had to push the pony between them. The wheels, rusty and without tyres, stuck in the ruts and on the enormous chalky stones. Sometimes when the wheels dug into the ground the pony stopped dead with his nose right down; at other times he seemed to paw the air with his forefeet.

At last they reached the top of the hill. They were over the worst. Their home was half-way down the slope on the other side and already they could see the chimneys. When they were only a few yards from their own gate, they saw a dog walking up the hill with a man. The man was their neighbour, Mr Richardson, who was so clever and worked in London at the museum.

'Hide!' hissed Cathy. 'No – it's too late. He's seen us.'

Anyway, there was nowhere to go. Nor could

Roger imagine why Cathy should want to hide from such an old friend.

'Hullo, what's this?' called Mr Richardson from a distance, waving his stick at the pony.

'Hold on,' said Cathy in a low voice to Roger. 'Don't let him have his head. He might shy.'

Roger frowned but did as she told him. It was clear that the pony seemed much more like a real one to Cathy than it did to Roger.

'Hullo, there!' repeated Mr Richardson, closer now. 'Where did you get that magnificent beast?'

'We found him wandering,' Cathy replied. 'He's lost his bridle. Well – you can see.'

Roger glanced at Cathy. She looked absolutely solemn, as though she meant every word she said. Mr Richardson seemed to realize that, too. He came near to the pony and put his hand on its proud black neck.

'Certainly I can see,' he agreed. 'And I can see that this is indeed the prince of beasts. But

37

the extraordinary thing is –' He broke off, shaking his head and clicking his teeth. He began to walk round the battered old pram, touching this and that and muttering all the time *Astonishing! Remarkable! A coincidence indeed!* At last he stopped and looked at them over his spectacles. 'You wouldn't care to sell me this contraption, I suppose?'

Somehow Cathy had half expected this; it was the reason she had wanted to hide.

'No, sorry, not for sale,' she said in a quick mumble. She had a dreadful feeling that he might seize the pram and wheel it quickly away, with the pony desperately prancing ahead. She hung on extra hard and began edging towards the gate of home. Once she was inside the pony would be safe.

'A pity,' said Mr Richardson almost wistfully. 'I'd pay you well. You could buy something else with the money. Isn't there something else you want badly?'

39

'We want a pony,' said Cathy, 'and we've got one.'

'This perambulator is many years old,' he explained. 'The people at the museum would be interested. We already have a collection of such things, but not one like this. . . . You are really quite sure?' And this time he turned to Roger, as though he might have more sense than a mere girl.

Roger shook his head dumbly. He did just wonder how much money Mr Richardson would be likely to pay for the pony; but he put the thought out of his mind as quickly as possible.

'Good-bye, Mr Richardson,' said Cathy. 'I hope you have a nice walk.'

'Yes – yes, thank you, my dear. I'm sure I shall. . . . Oh well, if you should ever change your mind. . . .'

'We'll let you know,' Roger said, nodding hard as he followed Cathy inside, 'when we get tired of it.'

Cathy ran through the garden with the pony and did not stop until she reached the orchard, where the grass was long and wet. She flung her arms round the pony's neck and cried angrily: 'How could you have said that? We'll never get tired of him!'

'You may not,' agreed Roger.

'Anyway, I gave Mrs Boddy my penny, not yours. So he's mine.'

'He's half mine,' Roger replied. 'When I can get change for my penny I'll give you a halfpenny.'

'Perhaps I won't take it.'

Roger decided to change the subject.

'What shall we call him?'

Cathy got into the pram and sat down, staring at the pony.

'Hero,' she suggested.

'No – Prince.'

'There are hundreds of horses called Prince.'

'Prince because he's black,' insisted Roger.

'And because he's brave. And because he's the prince of beasts. Prince Penny.'

'All right,' said Cathy. 'But don't forget what you owe me.'

By now the fine day had changed. The sun had gone and it was truly winter. Cathy and Roger decided that Prince Penny must be stabled. They led him in the direction of the garden shed. This had once been a cowshed and there was still one of the old stalls left. Their father always pushed the lawnmower in there. They cleared another space, and moved the lawnmower, and gave the stall to the pony. There was some straw in an empty box on a shelf. They spread the straw and then dashed off down to the orchard again and pulled some grass for him. All they could find for water was an enamel dish, but it was better than nothing.

'There,' said Cathy. 'That's done.' She slapped the pony in a loving way on his behind. 'I wish he had a bridle though.'

43

'What for?'

'So that we could take it off and hang it on a nail, of course,' said Cathy.

Suddenly she was filled with joy and pleasure at what they had brought home. Even if Prince Penny had had a real heart in his body, real blood in his veins and real breath to blow steamily above his head in the darkness of his stable, Cathy could hardly have felt happier than she did at that moment.

4

Holiday Time

Cathy grew so fond of Prince Penny that she began to wonder how she had ever managed without him. Roger liked him, too; but not in quite the same way. For weeks on end, the pony was all that Cathy needed to play with. Roger grew bored after a bit and began going off with his own friends. At first this made Cathy cross, but she soon found that she and Prince Penny got on very well without Roger.

'I'll give you back your halfpenny, if you like,' she said.

But he did not like. He did not want to give up the pony altogether.

Each morning before she went to school,

whatever the weather might be, Cathy dashed to the shed where Prince Penny was stabled, fed him and gave him fresh water and saw that he was quite comfortable. School was a good way away so she and Roger stayed to dinner. Cathy had to wait until the evening to see the pony again. Then she groomed him and exercised him.

As the spring came and the days grew longer, Cathy and the pony were able to go farther. They would gallop up the steep grassy slopes to the top of the downs, where you could see the sea. It was hard work pushing the pram in such steep places, but Cathy hardly gave it a thought; she had quite enough imagination to feel that it was the pony who did all the work.

'If you went as far as the wood,' her mother suggested one day, 'you could bring back some sticks for firelighting.'

So off went Cathy and Prince Penny, filled up

the pram with fallen wood and returned at a gallop.

Another day, their mother was in bed with a bad cold and Cathy and Roger did the shopping. They took the pony with them and the pram carried all the parcels easily. That time there was no boy on a bicycle to be rude about the pony.

'Any time the car breaks down,' their father told Cathy and Roger, 'I shall expect that pony of yours to take me to the station in time to catch the London train.'

Sometimes they took Prince Penny down to the lane below their home, where there was a very gentle slope, and took it in turns to ride in the pram – or the carriage, as it seemed then to be.

In this way the whole of the spring term went by. The Easter holidays arrived. At this time their grandmother sometimes came to stay.

'Granny wants us to go and stay with her this

year,' their mother told them. 'She thinks the sea air will do us good.'

'Oh good,' said Roger. 'When?'

'Next week. Perhaps Thursday.'

'All of us?'

'No. Daddy says he can't get away from the office just now. So Auntie Elaine has said she'll come here to look after him while we're away.'

'Then we shan't see her at Granny's.'

'She can't be in two places at once, that's certain.'

Roger nearly said *Oh Good* again. Their father's sister Elaine, who lived with Granny by the sea, was not a favourite aunt. She was extremely fussy, forever tidying up, and thus throwing away important things – like cereal packets waiting to be cut out, or scraps of newspaper with coupons you could send for free samples. Also she had extremely strong ideas about how little girls should behave. She would smile at Roger and say *Boys will be boys*. But to Cathy she would tell little stories that began *When I was your age*. Quite naturally, Cathy found this tiresome.

'You're very quiet, Cathy?' her mother said.

'Can I take the pony to Granny's?'

'How can you? Daddy's going to drive us down and bring Auntie Elaine back with him. You can't take the pony in the car.'

'Why can't I go by train?'

'Don't be silly, Cathy.'

'Then I don't want to go at all.'

'You know perfectly well how much you like going there. We'll only be away about a week. Surely you can do without your old pony for a little time like that?'

'I can't!' Cathy cried.

'I'm afraid you'll have to,' her mother said. 'I want to go and Roger wants to go, and Granny wants to have us. Also it will make a nice change for Elaine to come here. So you're the odd man out, Cathy.'

'I don't *want* to go away!'

'Please behave,' said her mother firmly.

Cathy was miserable. She was so miserable that Roger felt more sorry for her than cross with her for spoiling the fun of going away.

'We shan't be gone long,' he said, the day before they left, to comfort her.

'Too long. There'll be no one to feed Prince Penny. He'll starve.'

51

'Oh Cathy, how could he? He's only wood and plaster.'

'He doesn't seem like wood and plaster to me, and that's the important thing,' said Cathy. 'All the time I'm away I shall think of him starving and thirsting.'

Roger began to feel quite miserable in his turn. 'Can't you just leave him lots of extra grass,' he suggested, 'and a proper bucket of water? He'd be all right then.'

'I've got to hide him first,' Cathy said. She was wearing her furious face. 'We don't want anyone messing about with him.' Of course she meant their aunt.

Hiding Prince Penny took a whole afternoon. At the other end of the garden shed, away from the stall where Prince Penny was usually stabled, there was a kind of cupboard with its own door. In it was kept everything that was not really needed but which might come in useful one day – old tubs and flower vases,

broken deck-chairs, two garden forks with broken prongs, an old umbrella – really it was very much like the kind of old rubbish that Mrs Boddy turned out from time to time.

This seemed a good safe place to conceal the penny pony. For a start they had to clear out what was in there already. They made a clear space at the back of the shed, and they put Prince Penny in there, with plenty of straw, a whole sackful of grass, and a bucket of water. Then they put back the deck-chairs and the rest of the things, piling them up so that when the door was opened there was absolutely no sign of the pony.

'That'll do,' said Cathy. She began to look more cheerful.

The rest of the day was spent in packing and next morning the car was at the door and it was time to go.

At the very last minute, Cathy rushed to the

shed, put her head round the door and called good-bye to Prince Penny, though she could not see him.

Then she went back to the car and climbed in, and sat in her corner in glum silence for the whole journey.

5

By the Sea

Their grandmother lived in a small town by the
sea. Her house was tall and narrow, in a row of
other tall, narrow houses facing the sea front.
The house was painted white, with a black
shiny door and a brass knocker that gleamed in
the sun. It was an old house. When the wind
blew in off the sea all the windows rattled and
the rain beat against the glass till it seemed to be
almost inside the room. But during the Easter
holidays that year the weather was mostly fine,
though blowy. It was not nearly warm enough to
bathe, but it was warm enough to play about on
the beach.

One day, Cathy and Roger saw five people

riding their horses along the sands when the tide was low.

'There!' said Cathy. 'I could have galloped Prince Penny along the sands.'

'His wheels would have stuck,' said Roger.

Cathy did not reply. She never thought of the penny pony's wheels. She only thought of his beautiful arched neck, his proud nostrils and his fiery eyes.

Roger watched the riders longingly. Prince Penny was all right in a way, but Roger had not got over wanting a real pony, as Cathy seemed to have done. Cathy knew how to be happy with what she had got, but Roger still dreamt of what he could not have.

It was much more fun staying with Granny when Auntie Elaine was not there to fuss. Although Granny was so much older, she did not seem to mind the noise that Cathy and Roger made as they pounded up and down the stairs in that tall, thin house.

On the ground floor besides the hall and stairs was the dining-room and a little room that had been made into a kitchen; when the house was built the kitchen had been in the basement.

On the first floor was the drawing-room and Granny's bedroom. On the second floor was the bathroom and Auntie Elaine's bedroom where their mother slept during the visit, and a big linen closet with the hot water tank gurgling softly in one corner. And on the top floor were two small rooms with low sloping ceilings for Cathy and Roger.

'Let's go aloft, mate,' Roger would say. For the rooms were so high up they were like the crow's nest of an ancient ship, or like the very top of a lighthouse. In a strong wind the house seemed almost to sway; their mother said it was only the movement of the sea, heaving up and down, that made you feel that the house moved.

'Let's go below, mate,' Cathy would say in

her turn, after they had gazed out over the
waves from the front window, or over the
gardens of the next road from the back
window.

Then down they hurtled, down flight
after flight of stairs as fast as they could go,
swinging and thumping round each turn of
the banisters, until they came to the dark
basement.

It was cold and damp down there. On dull
days they needed a torch. The cellar and the
larder were right under the road and Cathy was
certain she could hear the sea roaring on the
other side of the wall.

'But the tide's out,' said Roger.

They poked about among the cobwebs in the
old silent kitchen. Cathy made enormous im-
aginary stews in a huge iron pot, and then
spread meals for twenty at a time on the big
wooden table that was so heavy they could not
move it.

'The whole family will be coming,' she would announce. 'I shall give them turkey.'

'Except for home,' Roger said again and again, 'this is the best place we know.'

He felt as though he would like to stay there for months and months. And if it had not been for Prince Penny Cathy would have felt the same.

'How I shall miss you!' their grandmother said one evening. 'It's been lovely having you

here. You must come again in the summer.
Promise me you'll come.'

'Yes, *please!*' they cried.

'And even if Daddy's too busy,' said Roger,
'Auntie Elaine could look after him again,
couldn't she?'

Their mother looked at them both in a
rather knowing way. Cathy and Roger thought
that she, too, had enjoyed this visit better than

any other they had made. She knew as well as they did that it was because their aunt was not there.

At last there was nothing for it but to go back home. Their father came down in the car to fetch them, bringing his sister with him. Roger was sad and disagreeable about it, but Cathy was full of a wild excitement that made her rush about and talk very fast at the top of her voice.

'That child's manners have not improved,' their aunt was heard to remark.

Soon they were all in the car, good-byes had been said, and Granny and Auntie Elaine stood outside on the pavement, waving as the car moved off.

'Enjoyed yourselves?' their father asked, as the car turned the corner and the waving ended.

'*Mm!*' said Roger.

'Cathy, too?' She did not reply, so he asked again – 'Did you enjoy yourself, Cathy?'

'Yes, thank you,' she said. 'How soon shall we be home?'

The journey seemed to go on for ever. They stopped for lunch and they stopped for tea. Where they had tea they bought postcards and wrote them to Granny, thanking her for having them to stay. Then they had to find a post office and buy stamps for the cards, and post them.

'What time is it?' Cathy kept asking. 'Shall we be back before dark?'

'What a fidget you are! Do stop fussing. We'll be back when we get there and not before.'

It was dusk when they drove in through the open gates and stopped the car just outside the garage. Almost before it had stopped, Cathy was out of the car.

'What's the matter with her?' she heard her father say, as she dashed off. And Roger replied, 'It's that pony.'

She heard no more. She was flying across the grass, ducking under the cherry tree that had

65

burst into flower while they were away. The garden shed seemed a mile from the house, but at last she reached it. She fumbled for the latch and pulled the door open. She wanted so much to see Prince Penny that she half expected him to be as keen himself and to whinny a greeting. She peered in through the shadows. It would be dark inside the shed, she knew, and she wished she had stopped long enough to pick up a torch.

But there was no need.

She knew at once that the shed was empty. It was a dim and shadowy cavern from which everything had gone – the tubs, the deck-chairs, the broken forks – and the penny pony.

6

Gone!

Cathy clapped her hands over her ears and screamed.

'Roger! Roger! *Roger!*'

He was helping to get the luggage out of the car, and he dropped the suitcase he was just dragging from the boot. It fell on his father's toe.

'Look out, you clumsy lout!' cried his father. His toe hurt so much it made him furiously angry.

'Sorry,' muttered Roger. It seemed a good moment to remove himself as fast as possible, and he went scurrying across the garden to the shed.

68

Cathy was standing by the open doorway. She had leant her arms against the doorpost and her head on them, and she was crying. She was doing more than just cry – she was sobbing with disappointment and shock and rage.

'He's gone!' she bellowed. 'He's gone – he's gone! Someone's taken him – some beastly person! Oh where is he – where is he? Oh what shall I do? Oh what can be happening to him without me to look after him? Oh Roger – oh Prince Penny – oh – oh – oh. . . .'

Roger peered into the black mouth of the shed. He had remembered to bring a torch. There was not much battery left, but even a small light showed him enough.

'It's empty,' he said.

'I know that, stupid. It's empty and the penny pony's gone for ever. . . .'

'But where, Cathy?'

'How do I know? If I knew, then it would be all right – I could just go and fetch him home.'

'Perhaps he's in the other end of the shed.'

'Why should he be?'

'He always used to live there,' Roger pointed out. 'Perhaps he didn't care for it down this end and so he's gone back to his stall.'

Cathy stopped crying and they went into the main part of the shed. That was tidy, too, with the two wheelbarrows standing side by side,

70

with bast and green string hanging neatly on hooks, and the spades and the forks and the trowels clean and shining, every one in its place and the floor swept. But in the stall where Prince Penny had once been stabled, the lawn-mower now stood.

The feeble light from Roger's torch wavered over the shed and then went out.

'Anyway, we've seen enough,' he said.

'Where is he?' wailed Cathy. 'Where is he?'

'Someone's been spring cleaning, I suppose,' said Roger gloomily. 'I don't see why people always want to be turning out.'

'*She* did it!' cried Cathy. 'That's who it was! It was *her!*'

'Do you mean –?'

'Auntie Elaine, of course! Just the sort of thing she *would* do!'

At this moment they heard their mother calling from the house.

'Where have you two gone? Cathy! Roger!

71

It's late. Come and have your supper and get to bed.'

Bursting with her tale of woe, Cathy rushed back to the house and flung herself on her mother.

'The pony's gone! The pony's gone! He's been tidied away and it was Auntie Elaine! She put him in the dustbin! He's gone! Oh how can we ever, ever get him back again?'

'Cathy, Cathy – for goodness' sake stop making such a noise! Tell me what it's all about.'

Between them they told how they had hidden the pony in the shed before they went away. First Cathy told a bit, then Roger told a bit, and before they were half-way through their father had come in and now was standing listening.

'Oh lawks!' he said when they had finished – and that usually made them laugh, but this evening they were not in the mood. 'Do you mean to tell me your precious pony was in the shed with all that old rubbish?'

'Yes he *was!* But where is he now?'

'Don't start again, Cathy!' her mother cried quickly. She looked at her husband in a rather reproachful way. 'I believe you know something about this, my dear,' she said.

'In a way, I'm afraid I do,' he agreed. 'Look, Cathy – look, Roger – I couldn't know Prince Penny was hidden in there, now could I?'

'You must have known he was somewhere, Daddy.'

'I thought he was in the old stall where I used to keep the mower. I haven't even been out to the shed since Elaine cleaned it all last week. . . .

'I knew she'd done it!'

'That'll do, Cathy. . . .'

'Look,' their father said, rubbing up his hair in the way he had when he was fussed. 'I'm terribly sorry about this – I really am. I'll tell you what happened. Miss Maltby came here asking for jumble – she was having another sale very suddenly – she'd heard of some animal she

74

wanted to buy and she had to get the money quickly. I told your aunt to see what she could find in the shed. I had no idea you'd put the pony in there, or of course I'd have been more careful.'

Cathy was quite pale with grief. The tears ran quietly down her cheeks. She was too sad even to sob, she just sniffed and sniffed. Her father pulled her into his arms – he even picked her up, though she was getting rather big for that – and tried to comfort her, to make her laugh, to think of some way to make things better.

But all she said was '*He's gone*' and more tears came to take the place of those that had already soaked themselves into the front of her jersey.

'When was the jumble sale, Daddy?' Roger asked.

'It was last Saturday.'

'Perhaps Prince Penny was left over at the end,' Roger suggested. 'Not many people would want him.'

76

'That's just a chance,' their mother said.

'Oh Daddy, please ring up Miss Maltby and ask – and ask. . . .'

But as luck would have it, there was no reply. Miss Maltby was either out for the evening, or what was more likely she was away in the fields somewhere, looking after one of her animals.

'We'll have to wait till the morning, Cathy. Cheer up. Roger's quite right, you know. Not everybody wants a pony of that particular kind.'

Miss Maltby Again

When Cathy woke next morning she thought at once about Prince Penny. She jumped out of bed and pulled on her clothes as fast as she could, then rushed downstairs without so much as brushing her teeth. She wanted to see about telephoning to Miss Maltby.

But as she reached the little cubby hole under the stairs where the telephone was kept, she found her father just hanging up the receiver. She heard him sigh. She knew then what he would have to tell her. Her heart sank down and down.

He smiled a little when he saw her. 'Good morning, Catherine.' He did not often call her

by her full name. She thought that he did so now to make her feel grown-up, so that she would not start crying again.

'Was it Miss Maltby?' she asked.

He nodded. 'I'm afraid the pony's gone, old girl. I'm so sorry about it. If I could only put it all right for you, but there seems no way. I feel an old beast about it, I can tell you that.'

'You didn't mean it to happen,' Cathy said. 'It was all because of –' she broke off, remembering that Auntie Elaine was his sister, after all, so he probably liked her very much.

'And try not to blame poor Elaine,' he said. 'She just thought the pony was part of the junk I had said she could turn out.'

Cathy did not reply. She turned back up the stairs and her mind was full of black thoughts about aunts.

'I should go and see Miss Maltby sometime today,' her father called after her. 'She's very upset, too.'

80

'Not her fault,' mumbled Cathy.

It was the last day of the holidays. It was fine
and warm, but it might just as well have been
pouring with rain. Roger wanted to go and see
Miss Maltby at once, because he still thought
they might find out who had bought the pony
and somehow get it back. But Cathy knew it
would be hopeless and she refused to talk about
it, or about Miss Maltby. It was the middle of
the afternoon before she began to weaken.

'We could just walk past her place,' Roger
said. 'If we see her we can ask her, and if we
don't see her we won't bother to look for
her.'

He turned at once in the direction of Miss
Maltby's home, and Cathy followed slowly. But
after a few yards she decided to catch him up.

Sure enough, as they reached her gate, they
saw Miss Maltby filling a bucket with water at
the pump in the stable yard. She was still wearing her green trousers, but as it was a warm day

she was wearing a red shirt instead of a sweater. But since her hair was the same colour winter or summer, Roger said she still looked like traffic lights round the wrong way.

The moment she saw them, Miss Maltby called out to them and dumped the bucket and came hurrying towards them.

'Oh Cathy dear, I'm so terribly sorry about the jumble. I didn't realize at all about that pram of yours being so precious.'

'It was a pony, not a pram,' said Cathy. 'It was what we bought from Mrs Boddy that day you let us clean out the hamsters.'

'Worse and worse!' cried Miss Maltby. 'The trouble was, you see, I had had a jumble sale so recently that it was difficult to find enough things for another one. I grabbed everything I could lay hands on, and your aunt was so kind and helpful.'

'Was she?' said Cathy.

'Did the sale go all right?' asked Roger politely, because he was really afraid of what Cathy might say next about their kind and helpful aunt.

'It went very well in the end,' Miss Maltby said. 'At first things were very slow and I got rather worried, because I wanted the money so badly. Then along came Mr Richardson and everything, as you know, was all right.'

'We don't know, as a matter of fact,' Roger said slowly. 'Did he buy a lot of things, then?'

'He bought one thing for a lot of money, Roger! Well, surely your father told you? It was your pony, as you call it, that Mr Richardson bought. It's going into his museum. He's over-joyed. And so, you can guess, am I.'

Cathy was looking at Miss Maltby as though she could hardly believe her ears.

'But he knew it was ours!' she cried. 'He asked if he could buy it ages ago, and we said no. He's a traitor!'

84

'If it was ages ago, I suppose he thought you'd got tired of it.'

'We did say if we ever got tired of it –' Roger began, but Cathy broke in furiously.

'He'll have to give it back!' she cried. 'Who-ever heard of a pony in a museum?'

Miss Maltby was beginning to look extremely worried. Everything had gone so well for her it must have been difficult for her to believe it could be going wrong now.

'If you want it back so much,' she said at last, 'I suppose I shall have to see what I can do. But let me show you something first.'

She turned and began walking back towards the pump. She picked up the bucket and went on past the house and the sheds to the little paddock by the orchard. In the paddock was a black pony. He was very thin. His bones stuck out under his shabby coat, and when he moved he went a little lame.

Miss Maltby made soft calling sounds and the

85

pony pricked his ears. He moved a step or two towards her, then stopped.

'Stand quite still,' Miss Maltby said quietly to Cathy and Roger. 'He's very nervy, but he's getting better every day. He's had a bad time. You might not think it, but he's put on a bit of fat already.'

'He's new, isn't he?' Roger asked.

'Yes, he is. I hope I'll be able to keep him. The thing is – he's the pony I bought with the money Mr Richardson paid for yours.'

In complete silence, Cathy and Roger stood there staring first at the pony and then at Miss Maltby, and then at the pony again.

Miss Maltby smiled. Very gently, very un-hurriedly, she went towards the black pony. With a slow, steady movement she raised her hand and held it out. Cathy and Roger saw that there was a lump of sugar on her open palm.

Gradually, step by doubtful step, the pony

came close. Then he stretched out his poor thin neck and his soft lip flipped at the sugar. Soon it was crunching between his great teeth. Miss Maltby gave him another lump. Then she stood absolutely still, waiting.

The pony stood flicking his tail, shifting his ears forward. He stamped and shivered. Then he moved. He came a step or two closer. Again he paused. Then he made two quick steps. He put his head down in a sudden quick butting movement, and rubbed it swiftly against Miss Maltby's shoulder. Then, as though overcome with shyness at what he had done, he swooped away in a quick semi-circle and went back across the paddock as fast as his lameness would let him.

'Soon he'll come when I call him. Soon he'll have a fine shining coat and bright eyes again,' said Miss Maltby. 'So long as I am able to keep him.'

Cathy leant on the paddock railing and

watched the pony. She thought a great many things.

'Is it really true,' she said at last, 'that because Mr Richardson bought our penny pony – this pony's got a home?'

'Yes, it's really true. Mr Richardson knew what I wanted the money for and he was very, very generous. He could have bought your pony for practically nothing, but he paid what he said it was worth to him. So I was able to buy this pony after all. Sometimes, as you know, I find other homes for my animals. But I want to keep this one. That is – if you'll let me.'

Cathy laughed suddenly. 'What a silly thing to say!'

'No. It isn't silly. Because in a way, he's more yours than mine.'

'Perhaps we could come and see him sometimes,' Cathy said. 'Could we?'

'I think he *is* yours,' Miss Maltby said, as

though she had come to a great decision. 'You can't keep a pony at home, I know. So I'll keep him here for you. And you can come and see him when you like. I'll show you how to groom him and feed him. In a few months he'll be ready for riding again.'

'We don't know how to ride,' faltered Cathy, her heart beating so fast she could hardly find any breath.

'I can teach you.'

'Then there's his keep – his food and everything. . . .'

'I daresay you wouldn't mind cleaning out the hamsters every now and again, would you?'

'Oh Miss Maltby!' cried Cathy. 'Oh Miss Maltby!'

Roger looked at her in disgust. 'She's going to cry,' he said. 'I don't know what's the matter with her. She cries all the time. It doesn't matter if you give her a pony or take one away. She still cries.'

'What's his name?' Cathy asked, ignoring Roger.

'He's called Prince. . . . Now what are you laughing at?'

They could hardly tell her, they were so filled with excitement and pleasure. At last Miss Maltby gave up trying to find out what it was all about. She caught their laughter, and they all three stood there, making such a noise that

Prince stood still in the middle of the paddock, and tossed his head in alarm. . . .

Later, when Cathy and Roger were rushing home with their wonderful news, Cathy remembered how they had gone home once before, pushing Prince Penny ahead of them, and feeling as though they had everything they could possibly want.

'We've got the best thing in the world now,' Roger was shouting, as he ran along behind Cathy. 'This time we really have. We've got everything in the world we need.'

'Except the penny pony,' Cathy said rather obstinately. 'But never mind. I'm sure he understands.'

About the Author

Barbara Willard went to a convent school, and then tried acting for a while. The theatre is still one of her greatest interests. Her first adult novel was published when she was 22, and she went on writing about one a year until the Second World War interrupted her.

After the war she went to live in the country, working for the story departments of major film companies and as a play reader. Her first children's book, *The House with Roots*, was published by Constable in 1959, and she gave up working for film companies when she settled down to writing children's books.

She is unmarried, and likes gardening, house-painting, driving, travel, cats and dogs, and cooking, eating and drinking.

Some other Young Puffins

Fantastic Mr Fox
Roald Dahl

Every evening Mr Fox would creep down into the valley in the
darkness and help himself to a nice plump chicken, duck or turkey,
but there came a day when Farmers Boggis, Bunce and Bean
determined to stop him whatever the cost . . .

Playtime Stories
Joyce Donoghue

Everyday children in everyday situations – these are stories for
parents to read aloud and share with their children.

Tales of Joe and Timothy
Joe and Timothy Together
Dorothy Edwards

Friendly, interesting stories about two small boys living in different
flats in a tall, tall house, and the good times they have together. By
the author of the *Naughty Little Sister* stories.

The Anita Hewett Animal Story Book

A collection of cheerful, funny, varied animal stories from all over
the world. Ideal for reading aloud to children of five or six.

The Shrinking of Treehorn
Florence Parry Heide

'Nobody shrinks!' declared Treehorn's father, but Treehorn *was*
shrinking, and it wasn't long before even the unshakeable adults
had to admit it.

The Young Puffin Book of Verse

Barbara Ireson

A deluge of poems about such fascinating subjects as birds and
balloons, mice and moonshine, farmers and frogs, pigeons and
pirates, especially chosen to please young people of four to eight.
(*Original*)

Adventures of Galldora

New Adventures of Galldora

Modwena Sedgwick

Galldora, the rag doll, has more hair-raising adventures. In this
book she saves Marybell and her father from drowning, and hides a
top-secret document from thieves after her first trip in an aeroplane.
Strangest of all, she saves the day when she is baked in a rabbit pie!

Tales from the End Cottage

More Tales from the End Cottage

Eileen Bell

Two tabby cats and a peke live with Mrs Apple in a
Northamptonshire cottage. They quarrel, have adventures and
entertain dangerous strangers. A new author with a special talent
for writing about animals. For reading aloud to five and over,
private reading seven-plus. (*Original*)

About Teddy Robinson

Joan G. Robinson

New adventures for the comfortable teddy bear and his friend
Deborah. Perfect bedtime reading for four-year-olds.

George

Agnes Sligh Turnbull

George was good at arithmetic, and housekeeping, and at keeping
children happy and well behaved. The pity of it was that he was a
rabbit so Mr Weaver didn't believe in him. Splendid for six-year-olds
and over.